The Flight of the NEZ PERCE

Highlights from American History

Illustrations by Dan White, Text by Bill Schneider

Design, illustrations, typesetting, and other prepress work by Falcon Press, Helena, Montana. Printed in Singapore.

Library of Congress Number 88-80227
ISBN 0-937959-39-1

The Mountain Indians

The Nez Perce were proud, intelligent Indians adapted to life in the mountains. They were energetic, religious, and hard-working. As hunters and fishermen, they were skillful. As warriors, they were unexcelled. As horsemen, they were the best.

They lived in what is now Idaho, eastern Oregon, and eastern Washington along the forks of the Clearwater, Salmon, and Snake rivers. However, they traveled widely, venturing west to the Cascade Range of western Oregon and western Washington and east over the Bitterroot Mountains into Montana. The Nez Perce had a fertile

homeland with rivers filled with fish, forests rich with game, and meadows thick with edible plants. And it was a place of sheer beauty.

Like other Indians, the Nez Perce had the deepest affection for their homeland. They compared the land to their mother because from it they grew. To them, their land was worth more than any amount of money. They did not pay for their land, nor would they sell it.

They wore full suits of clothes made from the skins of deer, elk, and bison. Their clothes were always clean and often carefully decorated and painted. They lived in cone-shaped huts in small villages along the banks of one of the many rivers in their homeland. Many villages also had "long houses" for ceremonies and meetings.

The men hunted large animals, while the women gathered berries and roots. Boys watched their fathers' horses and fished. Girls helped their mothers prepare food and clothing.

The Nez Perce lived on wild game—elk, deer, bison, and other animals. Plus, they used many plants in their diet—with their favorite being the root of the camas. They dug camas roots each spring and stored many for later use.

The annual salmon runs were also vital to their diet. The men and boys would spear, net, and catch many salmon. The women and girls would clean and then, smoke or dry them. When completely dried, the salmon looked like reddish-brown boards, but later in the year, when boiled, the salmon turned into a tasty meal.

In the early 1800s, white missionaries taught the Nez Perce to grow crops and raise livestock. The Nez Perce became experts at this, too, and before long, they grew much of their food, with both men and women helping to raise crops and livestock. They preferred fresh beef over dried bison meat that required dangerous, year-long hunts into the domain of the Blackfeet, Gros Ventre and Crow Indians.

The Nez Perce never tamed wild animals, but when they acquired horses in the early 1700s, they soon became skilled horsemen. They bred horses and developed a new breed now known as Appaloosa.

They were friendly to members of the Lewis and Clark Expedition when it passed through Idaho in 1805, and they took care of the explorers' horses while they canoed down the Snake and Columbia rivers to the Pacific Ocean. In their journals, Lewis and Clark favored the Nez Perce among the tribes they encountered on their famous expedition.

The Nez Perce fought with other tribes, but major battles were rare. The Nez Perce occasionally battled with other tribes over territorial rights to hunt bison. Most other raids made by the Nez Perce were limited to horse-stealing. Actually, horse-stealing was a favorite challenge to the Nez Perce, and a young warrior could prove his skill and bravery with several successful horse-stealing raids on other tribes.

The Nez Perce traded with other tribes more often than fighting with them. Since the Nez Perce always had many horses, they often traded them to other tribes for buffalo robes, guns, tools, and other important items.

Until the mid-1800s, life was good for the Nez Perce. They had permanent villages with fine lodges. They grew crops and raised cattle for food. They had enough of everything, and they were at peace with themselves, other tribes, and their environment.

Then, white settlers moved into the land of the Nez Perce.

White Neighbors

Missionaries were the first whites to come to Nez Perce country. The Nez Perce learned much from the missionaries, and the traditional life style of the mountain Indians began to change.

Then, more whites came—miners, ranchers, farmers, and others. The Nez Perce tried to live in harmony and learn from their new white neighbors. In fact, the Nez Perce probably lived peacefully with their white neighbors longer than most Indian tribes. Even though whites—especially miners—trespassed and claimed parts of the Nez Perce homeland, the Nez Perce tolerated them and tried to adjust to the new way of life. They endured ridicule and violent crimes against their people—and still avoided the warfare that had led to the destruction of other Indian tribes.

Even when the intruders dug up the beautiful streams, cut the forests, and let their farmers' pigs eat the beloved crops of wild camas and other edible roots. . . even when the intruders settled on the most fertile parts of the Nez Perce homeland. . . even when treaties and agreements were broken. . . even when whites murdered tribal members, the Nez Perce did not fight. Instead, they tried hard to live in peace with their new neighbors. At times, the Nez Perce actually traded and had other business dealings with the settlers.

The Nez Perce thought the miners would dig gold for a few years and be gone. They thought the settlers would get tired of cold mountain winters and move on. But they were wrong.

In 1855, an enormous council was held between the U.S. Government, represented by Governor Stevens, and the Nez Perce and many other tribes—the Cayuses, Yakimas, Umatillas, and Walla Wallas. Five thousand Indians crowded into a grassy plain along the Walla Walla River. The tribes had all their chiefs there—Looking Glass, Spotted Eagle, Yellow Serpent, Red Wolf, Eagle-from-the-light, James, Lawyer, Timothy, and of course, the elder Joseph.

The U.S. Government offered a treaty that created three large reservations for the tribes. The tribes accepted the treaty and moved to their reservations.

Unfortunately, a few years later, gold was discovered on the Nez Perce reservations, and thousands of miners moved in, violating the treaty. Old Joseph complained again and again, but the U.S. Government would not remove the trespassers.

The Nez Perce watched the intruders take more and more of their reservation, but Old Joseph remained diplomatic and tolerant. He appealed to government leaders, but the trespassing continued.

One day, Old Joseph took his sons, Joseph and Ollokot, aside and told them that this land was like their mother—something the white man would never understand. "You ask me to dig for stone. Shall I dig under the skin for her bones? You ask me to cut the grass and make hay and sell it and be rich like white men. But dare I cut off my mother's hair?"

Old Joseph was dying, and he feared for his people and their land. "My son. . . ," he told Joseph, "you are the chief. . . Always remember that your father never sold his country. You must stop your ears whenever you are asked to sign a treaty selling your home. A few years more, and the white man will be all around you. They have their eyes on your land. My son, never forget my dying words. This country holds your father's body. Never sell the bones of your father and your mother."

Joseph was still young—only thirty-one. But now, he was chief. He buried his father in the beautiful valley of the winding river, the Wallowa Valley, and promptly took up his father's debate to keep this land for his people.

Miners had already set

up camp on much of the Nez Perce reservation. Fortunately, no gold was discovered in the Wallowa Valley, but cattlemen wanted the lush grass and started moving into the last of the Nez Perce land.

No land was sacred to the white man. No treaty was honored. No complaint by Joseph was heard.

Old Joseph and the other Nez Perce chiefs had given up most of their homeland to live on a reservation. Then, whites moved onto the reservation, so the Nez Perce gave up much of the reservation, moving to the last valley, the Wallowa Country, the land of the winding river. But then, in 1877, even that valley was opened to white settlers by the U.S. Government, and young Joseph and his people were ordered out of the valley and onto another reservation too small to allow the Nez Perce to live the way they had for ages. For obvious reasons, the Nez Perce called this new agreement the "steal treaty."

The Nez Perce did not want violence, but the Government almost forced them to fight.

General Howard moved his troops into the Wallowa Valley in anticipation of a war with the Nez Perce. But still, Joseph did not want to fight, and he requested one last meeting

with the General. But the General seemed tired of talk. He ordered the Nez Perce off the land and gave them only thirty days to move.

The Nez Perce chiefs objected, but after much thought and discussion, they decided to obey the order. They started rounding up their horses and abandoning their lodges. Soon, they started moving to their new and pitifully small home.

Leaving the valley of the winding river was very difficult. The Nez Perce were heartbroken and bitter. It took only one small incident to crack the forced and unpopular peace.

Two young warriors riding double on a horse let their mount get out of control and trample food gathered by one of the women. The woman's husband scolded them bitterly, claiming they were "playing brave" and destroying his family's food supply when they should be out avenging the crimes committed by whites, such as the murder of the father of one of the young warriors. The scolded warrior thought about this and then, at dawn, left with two others and went on a murderous raid.

The young warriors killed several white settlers. When they came back to camp and announced their crimes, another larger raiding party left, killing more settlers.

The frustration of trying to live with their white neighbors for many years had finally boiled over, and the Nez Perce War had begun.

The War Begins

General Howard quickly heard the stories of the deadly raids and immediately sent Captain Perry and about ninety troopers and a few civilian volunteers to the Nez Perce camp at White Bird Canyon. However, when Perry reached the Nez Perce camp, the Indians were waiting.

In the short but fierce battle, the Nez Perce used Indian fighting techniques and quickly had Perry's men on the run. The soldiers panicked and retreated as quickly as possible. About 34 whites died with no Indian casualties.

Thus, the first real battle of the war, the Battle of White Bird

Canyon, went down as a victory for the Nez Perce. In fact, it was so one-sided that it has been compared to the Battle of the Little Big Horn where General Custer died at the hands of the Sioux.

In the following days, there were several minor fights. In most, the Nez Perce won. Then came the Battle of the Clearwater.

The Nez Perce went up against General Howard and five hundred soldiers and civilian volunteers, and the Nez Perce chose to retreat. They did not suffer many casualties, but they were forced to quickly flee and leave behind most of their belongings, including treasures that had been in their families for generations.

After the Battle of the Clearwater, on July 12, 1877, General Howard made his biggest mistake. He did not chase down the Nez Perce and force a complete surrender. Instead, he gave Chief Joseph and his people time to leave their homeland and head east up the Lolo Trail, through the Bitterroot Mountains, and into the buffalo country of the Crows in what is now Montana.

The Nez Perce started up the Lolo Trail on July 16, four days after the Clearwater Battle, and General Howard started his pursuit on July 30. This launched one of the greatest adventures in American history—the flight of the Nez Perce.

The Historic Chase

The Nez Perce also made a big mistake. They assumed that once they abandoned their beloved homeland the war was over.

When the Nez Perce reached Lolo Creek in the Bitterroot Valley, they were confronted by a small group of soldiers led by Captain Rawn. The soldiers had blockaded the path down Lolo Creek, so the Nez Perce set up camp. They were not in a hurry, and several days passed as the Indians talked and even traded with the white settlers and troops. Historical records differ on what exactly happened at Lolo Creek, but most accounts give credit to the Nez Perce for talking their way out of a fight. Thus, the blockade has been called Fort Fizzle.

While a few Nez Perce negotiated with Captain Rawn, the main Indian force secretly passed around the point. They headed south down the Bitterroot Valley towards the Big Hole Basin. Along the way, they peacefully dealt with white settlers in several small towns. They traded with white businessmen, convincing many whites that the runaway Indians were not dangerous. Because of their friendly relations with the settlers in the area, the Nez Perce became even more relaxed and unconcerned.

Normally, the Nez Perce were very watchful and aware of everything happening around them. They would send out advance scouts to check for danger ahead and send back a rear guard to watch the back trail. But this time, they were convinced of their safety—a tragic error in judgment.

Young Looking Glass, son of the famous Nez Perce war chief with the same name, had been given command of the fleeing Indians. And it was Looking Glass who was primarily responsible for this and other bad decisions made during the historic retreat.

Unknown to the Nez Perce, Colonel Gibbon and about 150 troopers were hot on their trail, traveling twice as fast as the unhurried Indians. Gibbon considered the Nez Perce the enemy, and the only thought in his mind was to overtake and destroy the Nez Perce.

When the Nez Perce reached the Big Hole Basin, they liked what they found—a mostly unsettled valley resembling the wilderness setting of their abandoned home in Idaho. So they set up a good camp and decided to stay a few days. They were not in a hurry, not thinking about fighting, and not aware of disaster rapidly approaching.

The Nez Perce were vulnerable to surprise attack, and Colonel Gibbon did exactly that. He carefully and secretly scouted the Indian camp. Then, on August 9, 1877, as the first gray streaks of dawn shot through the sky, his troops surrounded the camp, waiting for daylight, to strike.

A lone Indian rose early on that morning and accidentally wandered into the waiting troops. He was instantly killed. The gunfire awoke the rest of the camp, but it was almost too late.

Gibbon had not planned to take any prisoners, even though the camp contained many women and children. He had ordered his soldiers to fire low into the tepees to kill the Indians in their sleep. The early riser may have saved the camp from complete disaster, but still many Indians died in the first volley of shots, including Chief Joseph's wife and many of the greatest Nez Perce warriors.

The Nez Perce reacted to the attack with the speed of lightning. They did not panic. Instead, the warriors grabbed their guns and scattered into the woods. As the soldiers rushed into the camp, the Nez Perce rushed out.

Then, the enraged warriors turned on the soldiers. They wanted revenge, and they fought with a fury that shocked even the experienced

Colonel Gibbon. Later, he exclaimed in disbelief at how the completely surprised Nez Perce could recover so quickly and put up such a fierce fight.

For five hours of furious fighting, the battle could have gone either way. But then, the Nez Perce—in their determination to avenge the deaths of their families—began to gain ground on their attackers.

Soon thereafter, Gibbon rode into the battle and ordered a retreat. Many of his troops were killed during this retreat. Gibbon himself was wounded as his horse was shot out from under him. The troops quickly fell back, many of them fearing a fate similar to General Custer's command, which had been completely wiped out.

Actually, the Nez Perce could have destroyed every last soldier, but now that they were jolted back into reality, they feared for the very survival of their people. They expected reinforcements to join Gibbon's beaten troops, and they were right. General Howard was rapidly marching down the Bitterroot Valley, hoping to catch up with Gibbon before he engaged the Nez Perce.

Thus, the Nez Perce left a few warriors to keep Gibbon's troops pinned down—a siege that lasted another twenty hours. The rest of the Indians quickly buried their dead, cared for the wounded, gathered their belongings, and headed up the Ruby Valley towards Yellowstone National Park.

A strong sense of survival now ruled the Nez Perce. They knew that for every white soldier they killed, a thousand would take his place. But for every warrior they lost, none would take his place. So they fled the Big Hole Valley fully aware that the fighting was not over.

The Nez Perce not only escaped the ambush at the Battle of the Big Hole, but they are considered the winner by many historians. However, it was a costly victory. Many Nez Perce fell in the valiant fight. Plus, the soldiers shot many women and children. Most families were disrupted. And the many wounded slowed down the progress of the escape.

Survivors of Gibbon's force told of the sorrowful wailing that swelled up from the Nez Perce camp when the fighters returned and saw so many of their loved ones dead and wounded. For the Nez Perce, the Battle of the Big Hole was a most bitter lesson.

The Great Escape

All thoughts of the war being over had left the minds of the Nez Perce. Under the new leadership of Chief Joseph and Chief Lean Elk, the Indians fled as rapidly as possible. They knew the soldiers would follow.

Now, they considered all whites their enemies, and on the way to Yellowstone Park, they met several white settlers, miners, ranchers, and others. The Nez Perce left some whites unharmed. But at Horse Prairie, the Nez Perce killed three ranchers and stole a large herd of horses. At Bannack, they confronted a large group of white settlers, but left without a fight. At Birch Creek, they attacked a wagon train and killed several whites.

Then, the Nez Perce headed farther south and set up camp at Camas Meadows. At the same time, General Howard set up camp less than a day's march away.

Both General Howard and the Nez Perce had scouts out, so both knew the other's position. That night, the Nez Perce chiefs met and decided to raid Howard's camp and steal his horses. Without horses,

Howard would not be able to keep up with the rapidly fleeing Nez Perce and their large supply of fresh ponies.

The raid was, in part, successful. The Nez Perce raiders silently crept into Howard's camp and cut many horses from the picket lines. However, they did not finish their raid before a sentry discovered them.

The Nez Perce drove the horses away while the soldiers scrambled to organize a pursuit. At dawn and still hurrying away from Howard's camp, the Nez Perce were shocked—and embarrassed—to see that they had stolen mostly mules and only a few horses. However, other horses had been cut loose and chased from Howard's camp.

Soon, at the edge of Camas Meadows, the soldiers caught up and a small skirmish followed. Neither side suffered many casualties, but the soldiers could not recover the mules and horses.

The Nez Perce did not consider the raid a great success, but it did slow Howard's progress. Without mules to carry supplies, he could not catch the Nez Perce, who moved into Yellowstone Park.

Howard had sent Lieutenant Bacon and a small command to intercept the Nez Perce at Targhee Pass which was on the way to Yellowstone Park. But Bacon arrived there too early. He did not see any sign of the Indians, so he left Targhee Pass. If he had remained there, he probably would have met the Nez Perce, possibly buying enough time to allow General Howard's forces to overtake the Indians.

Instead, Chief Joseph's band passed into Yellowstone Park and up the Madison River, through the Lower Geyser Basin along the Firehole River, over Mary Mountain and into the Yellowstone River valley north of Yellowstone Lake. During their stay in the Park, they took several park visitors prisoner but released them unharmed. Also, they had scouts out in every direction. The information they gathered from all these sources revealed to the Nez Perce that a trap had been set for them.

General Howard was again coming fast from the rear with 600 fighting men. Colonel Sturgis had set up a blockade on the Clark Fork of the Yellowstone River just beyond the present northeast entrance to the park. Farther south, Colonel Hart and his forces blocked exit from the park up the Shoshone River, now the east entrance to the park. Plus, Indian scouts loyal to Howard were closely tracking the location of the Nez Perce.

This was a huge assembly of military power in the remote region, and it seemed impossible for the Nez Perce to escape. But they did.

The Nez Perce deceived Colonel Sturgis into believing that they had chosen the southern exit and were heading for Colonel Hart's stand. Military scouts were constantly on the Nez Perce trail, so the Indians made an abrupt turn south toward the Shoshone River and Hart's troops. The scouts quickly reported this new route to the military. But then, the Nez Perce temporarily concealed their trail by driving their horses in every direction over a large area. Then, they doubled back and turned abruptly north toward the Clark Fork. By the time the military realized what was happening, the Nez Perce had escaped.

Receiving information from the scouts that the Nez Perce had headed south, Sturgis abandoned his post on the Clark Fork of the Yellowstone River and left to help Hart engage the Nez Perce. Thus, he made the escape possible.

While Sturgis headed south, the entire Nez Perce force—all 700 men, women and children, plus hundreds of horses—silently rushed single file down narrow canyons and through dense timber, hidden from all eyes, into the Clark Fork of the Yellowstone. They hurried over the Absaroka Range at Beartooth Pass, continuing down the Clark Fork until they reached the present-day site of Laurel, Montana, leaving more than a thousand frustrated soldiers far behind.

Some observers considered this escape almost supernatural. But in reality, the Indians had simply outsmarted the military.

The Clark Fork of the Yellowstone had actually been the Nez Perce's destination all along. They had hunted buffalo there, and they had developed a long-time relationship with the Crow Indians in the vicinity. They expected the Crows to help them, just as they had expected help from the Flatheads and Bannocks. But the Crows refused to help. This shocked and angered the Nez Perce, who could not understand why other Indians would help the white soldiers.

Sturgis and Howard both rapidly pursued the Nez Perce with Sturgis taking the lead. Sturgis caught the Nez Perce at Canyon Creek after days of hard marching. The soldiers were able to see the Nez Perce caravan scurrying away less than two miles away.

Faced with this danger, the Nez Perce chiefs sent back a small force of warriors to engage Sturgis and his forces. Even though the Indians were greatly outnumbered, they were able to hold off Sturgis and allow the rest of their people to escape again. At one time, only one Nez Perce warrior remained to fire at the pinned-down troops.

Actually, the military's Indian scouts—both Bannocks and Crows—more effectively pursued the Nez Perce and caused more damage to the fleeing Indians than the soldiers did. The scouts would catch and engage the back of the retreating Nez Perce force—and then run. The larger Nez Perce force could have easily crushed the small number of

Indian scouts, but they could not afford the time to fight—and let Sturgis and his troops catch up.

The Nez Perce fled north as fast as possible—through the Musselshell Valley, over Judith Gap by the Snowy Mountains and down to the Cow Island ford on the Missouri River. Here, they stole supplies stored for white settlers and soldiers and continued north to the Bear Paw Mountains, the site of their last fight.

The Last Stand

Although Chief Joseph was considered the leader of the runaway band of Nez Perce, he was merely one of many chiefs in control of the fleeing Indians. Even though young Chief Looking Glass had made earlier mistakes, he again influenced the other chiefs to make another bad decision.

Looking Glass was convinced that no soldiers were in close pursuit, so he slowed the pace for several days before camping in the Bear Paw Mountains. He was responsible for setting up camp in mid-day instead of forging ahead to the freedom of the Canadian border, only about forty miles away.

The Nez Perce camped on Snake Creek in the Bear Paw Mountains. Some warriors urged the chiefs to continue on to safety, even though the elders and children were weary from the long retreat and needed rest. Instead, the chiefs decided to camp, rest, and dine on fresh bison meat from a recent hunt.

As Chief Looking Glass believed, Howard and Sturgis had been left far behind, but unknown to the Nez Perce, another force led by Colonel Miles was rapidly approaching from the east. Miles surprised the Indians and cut them off from their horses. A few Indians escaped, but most were trapped.

With no horses, retreat was out of the question, so the Nez Perce dug pits and trenches and started a long siege. Many lives were lost on both sides. Five Nez Perce chiefs were slain—Looking Glass, Hahtalekin, Lean Elk, Toohoolhoolzote, and Ollokot, Joseph's brother.

The siege went on for six days. At one point, Joseph agreed to a short truce so he could meet with Miles, but Miles broke his word and took Joseph captive. Fortunately, the Nez Perce were able to capture one of Colonel Miles' lieutenants shortly thereafter and exchange him for Joseph.

The Nez Perce held out day after day hoping for help from Chief Sitting Bull and the Sioux who were camped just over the Canadian border. But when Sitting Bull received pleas for help from the Nez Perce, he moved his tribe in the other direction instead of helping Chief Joseph. No Indian brother, it seemed, would help the Nez Perce.

Miles had the Nez Perce surrounded. And then, General Howard arrived with part of his troops. The Indians were already starving and freezing in the October cold. There was no hope, but many warriors feared the terms of surrender. They distrusted the white soldiers and worried about bad treatment and even executions. After much discussion, however, Miles convinced the Nez Perce that they would be treated fairly and be returned to their homeland in Idaho in the spring. With that assurance, Chief Joseph and his warriors agreed to lay down their guns and end the fifteen-hundred-mile search for freedom.

On October 5, 1877, Chief Joseph proudly rode up to Colonel Miles, handed him his rifle, and made this famous speech:

"Tell General Howard I know his heart. What he told me before I have in my heart. I am tired of fighting. Our chiefs are killed. Looking Glass is dead. The old men are all killed. It is the young men who say yes or no. He who led the young men [Ollokot] is dead. It is cold and we have no blankets. The little children are freezing to death. My people, some of them, have run away to the hills and have no blankets, no food; no one knows where they are, perhaps freezing to death. I want time to look for my children and see how many of them I can find. Maybe I shall find them among the dead. Hear me, my chiefs, I am tired; my heart is sick and sad. From where the sun now stands, I will fight no more forever."

In response, Miles said, "No more battles and blood. From this sun, we will have a good time on both sides, your band and mine."

And the flight of the Nez Perce came to a sorrowful end.

More Broken Promises

After the surrender in the Bear Paws, Chief Joseph and his band of survivors considered Colonel Miles their protector. They expected the terms of the surrender agreed upon in the Bear Paws to be upheld by the U.S. Government, but they were wrong again.

The Nez Perce agreed to lay down their guns when Miles promised them they could return to Idaho in the spring following their historic flight. But instead, they were escorted to a series of military forts and severely mistreated along the way. They were marched long distances. They were floated down the icy Yellowstone River on flatboats, one of which capsized and drowned several Nez Perce. They were loaded on wagon trains and packed in railroad boxcars. And then, they were exiled at the Quapaw Reservation in Kansas.

Miles used all his influence to avoid this betrayal of the trust he had given Chief Joseph in the Bear Paws, but he was overruled. White settlers and politicians in the Northwest did not want the "renegade" Nez Perce to return, and they convinced their congressmen to oppose the terms of the surrender.

All along the way to Kansas, Chief Joseph strongly protested the unexpected exile. When his people finally realized they might never see their mountain home again, they were heartbroken. And Joseph simply asked, "When will the white man learn to tell the truth?"

The climate in Kansas differed so dramatically from their mountain homeland that the Nez Perce could not adapt to it. On top of that, whites in charge of the exiled Nez Perce failed to provide adequate shelter, food, or medical care. As a result, many Nez Perce died trying to survive the new, harsh environment.

Miles went to Joseph to explain. "You must not blame me," he told the leader of the Nez Perce. "I have endeavored to keep my word, but the chief who is over me has given the order, and I must obey it or resign. That would do you no good. Some other officer would carry out the order."

Chief Joseph did not blame Colonel Miles, but he could not understand a government that would not keep its word. Nor did he understand that the government considered the runaway Nez Perce criminals. The government rarely considered the desires of criminals.

Joseph continued his diplomatic efforts to return to the Northwest. In 1879, he was able to convince the government that his people could not stay on the Quapaw Reservation. But instead of allowing the Nez Perce to return to Idaho, the government offered them a tract of land on the Oakland Reservation in Oklahoma. Joseph accepted this compromise, but the new home was not much better than the one they left in Kansas.

So Chief Joseph kept up his political efforts to return to the mountains. And finally, after seven years in Kansas and Oklahoma, he succeeded.

The military had assumed that sooner or later the Nez Perce would adapt to the hot, flatland environment. But after so many Nez Perce had died and after the tribe had fallen into extremely poor health and economic despair, the government realized its mistake in locating the tribe in Kansas and Oklahoma. Most newborn babies, young children, and older tribal members had died, with Joseph's daughter among the dead. To keep the Nez Perce out of the mountains would mean death to all who surrendered at the Bear Paws.

Joseph had talked to many "Great White Chiefs," but he could not

get help for his people. "I have heard talk and talk, but nothing is done," Joseph complained. "Good words do not last long until they amount to something. Words do not pay for my dead people. They do not pay for my country, now overrun with white men. They do not protect my father's grave."

Joseph's pleas to government officials obviously brought no results, but then he started talking to reporters. He was interviewed by several newspapers and magazines, and he wrote articles for some of them.

His eloquent pleas and reviews of the Nez Perce war and long flight caught the public's eye. More and more people strongly favored ending the punishment and returning Chief Joseph's people to the mountains. Politicians received so much public pressure to help the Nez Perce that they overruled the northwestern congressmen who still opposed the return of the Nez Perce. Thus, in the spring of 1885, the 268 Nez Perce who had survived the seven-year exile returned to the mountains.

It was a victory for Chief Joseph, but not a complete victory. The exiled Nez Perce were split, with approximately half going to the Lapwai Reservation in Idaho and Chief Joseph and the other half going to the Colville Reservation in northern Washington. Shortly after arriving at Colville, Joseph noticed that the nearby Nespelem Valley looked more promising and asked to move there. This move was approved, and his band relocated once more in the summer of 1886.

The Nespelem pleased Joseph, and his people prospered there. Joseph married twice to two widows of warriors who died in the long flight for freedom. He was fairly content raising his children and his horses, but he kept trying to return to the Wallowa. He even traveled to Washington, D.C., to meet with President Theodore Roosevelt. But he could not win his last battle. He could not return to the valley of the winding river where the bones of his father and mother were buried.

On September 21, 1904, Chief Joseph died. A doctor from the Indian agency reported that he had died of a broken heart while sitting before his tepee fire.

Even though he and his people had suffered many injustices, he died with no hatred within him. He had stopped the killing, but he had never stopped fighting for his people, using words instead of bullets. He will always be remembered as a great leader. He was usually outranked and outnumbered, but never outclassed.

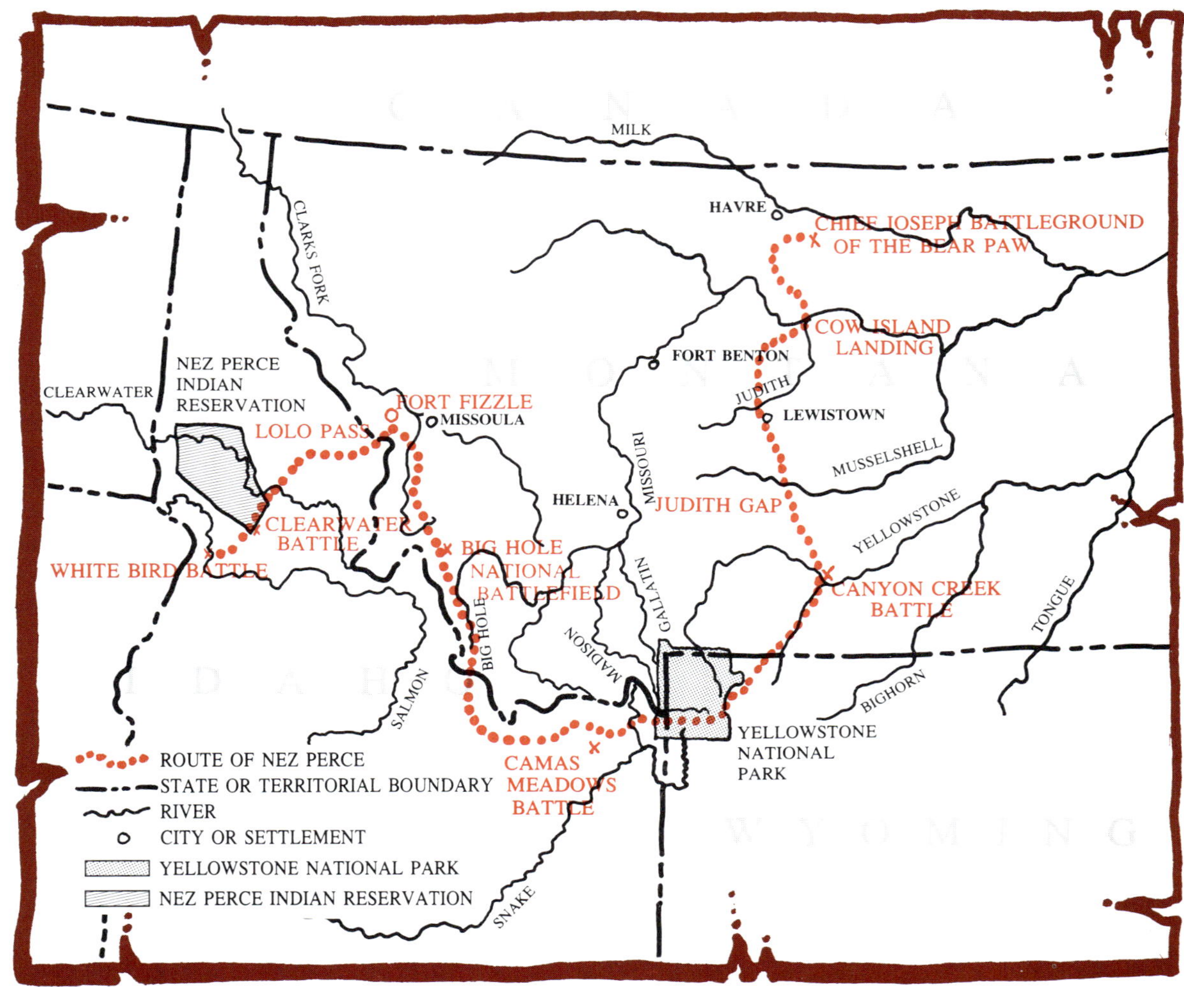

In Chief Joseph's Footsteps

Chief Joseph and his people traveled more than a thousand miles in their quest for peace and freedom. Although more than a hundred years have passed since then, the sad and difficult journey has not been forgotten. Along the route the Nez Perce followed, state, federal and tribal agencies have erected monuments to mark the sites of battles between the Nez Perce and the U.S. Army. The entire route has been declared a national historic trail, and plans are being made to develop parts of it for walking tours. At the Big Hole National Battlefield near Wisdom, Montana, visitors can roam through a museum, watch a slide program and follow self-guided walking trails around the battleground. Through the efforts of many, history buffs of today can re-live the flight of the Nez Perce.

For more information about the Nez Perce

Nez Perce National Historical Park
P.O. Box 93
Spalding, ID 83551
(208) 843-261

Nez Perce Tribal Headquarters
P.O. Box 305
Lapwai, ID 83540
(208) 843-2253

Big Hole National Battlefield
P.O. Box 237
Wisdom, MT 59761
(406) 689-3155

The Yellowstone Association
P.O. Box 117
Yellowstone National Park, WY 82190
(307) 344-7381

Colville Indian Agency
P.O. Box 150
Nespelen, WA 91155
(509) 634-4711

Idaho State Historical Society
610 N. Julia Davis Dr.
Boise, ID 83702
(208) 334-3356

Montana Historical Society
225 N. Roberts
Helena, MT 59620
(406) 444-2694

Highlights from American History

This book is only a start. It is the first in a series of similar children's books being published by Falcon Press.

This series, Highlights from American History, will contain brief versions of some of the most famous developments in American history. These stories are not only important and educational, but interesting. And now, they will be more available as Falcon Press develops this series of books.

The books have been written for readers ages 8-12. They can also be read to younger children.

For more information on future editions in the series, write Falcon Press, P.O. Box 1718, Helena, MT 59624.